A Symmetrically Tentacled Friendship

Thomas K Slee

Refraction Publishing

Contents

A Symmetrically Tentacled Friendship

Glixor hit pause. Humphrey Bogart's face, captured in crisp black and white, filled his TV screen. Bogart had no mandibles, no jowl flaps. He didn't even have antennae! And yet, Glixor could feel Bogart's pride in his gut. Feel it so keenly, burning just beneath the surface, that he knew Bogart would step up, do the right thing. The honourable thing, even though it would break his single human heart.

The paused scene reflected off the water that filled Glixor's viewing cavern, ripples washing the damp stone and algae in an eerie silver light that made the cables that powered his TV, VCR and dictaphone seem to vanish into the aether.

He dipped back below the water and flushed his gills. Only his optical membranes protruded above the surface. He hit play, and with a tentacle wrapped around the remote's waterproof casing, he let Casablanca's final scene play out. The credits rolled and the music swelled, filling his cavern with lush strings. He closed his membranes, pressed his suckers into the mossy sandstone and just... absorbed the music. Moments like this, he could almost imagine he was here by choice.

The tape screeched, then clunked. The movie over, his TV went black and Glixor sagged.

Rewind.

Pause.

He hauled himself back out of the water and carefully dried his tentacle tips before rifling through his notes. *...doesn't amount to a mountain of beans... mountain*? That couldn't be right. *mound,* maybe? Or *hill*? Humans were so strange, the movies they made even stranger, which only made him love them more.

He cleared the water from his gills, exercising his mandibles as he made his final annotations and huddled down over his microphone. He sucked in his jowl flaps in an attempt to match Bogart's clipped, sardonic delivery, and pressed record.

Bogart and Claude Rains fell into lockstep, and the camera tracked them as they strolled down the runway, into the fog. Glixor's practiced, melodic warble matched Bogart's word for word.

"... but it doesn't make a difference to our bet. You still owe me ten thousand credits."

Glixor relaxed and opened his chest. Rains' voice was a little softer. Rounder, but still slow as a boulder. Nothing like the spritely whistles and chitters of his own tongue.

"That ten thousand credits should pay our expenses."

"*Our* expenses?"

"Mmmm?" Glixor twisted his mandibles into a knowing smile.

"Louis, I think this is the beginning of a symmetrically tentacled friendship."

The credits rolled once more, and Glixor furrowed his gills. Something about that last line didn't sit right. He played it back, flicked through his notes. He just couldn't put a sucker on it.

Flaxnar would know. It was almost lunchtime anyway. He dropped his notes on his table, taking care to keep them dry and flopped over the water's edge. The water was warm and in it his body swelled, gravity no longer dragging him flat as it did on land. With a tenticular pulse, he swam down to the iron grill that barred his cavern entrance.

Crusted over with barnacles and algal growth, and jutting from the sandstone wall, the grill was a jarring reminder of his daily reality. Up in his cavern, his membranes glued to his TV screen as Humphrey Bogart saved the day, it was possible to forget. At least for a little while. He glared at the little red light, flashing incessantly, willing it to turn green

"Come on!" He whistled, low enough that the guard-anemone wouldn't be able to hear. What were they waiting for? The feeding shaft had just been filled. He could smell the unfiltered water, rich with moulds and contaminants, exotic flavours and mysterious particles, seeping down from the world above.

An electronic hum fizzed the water. Green light flooded the tunnel and the grill ground open. He jetted out, sweeping his tentacles in a graceful arc and dove down into the grotto.

The grotto was an ironic name, coined by Flaxnar. It was little more than a dingy common cavern, roughly hewn from grey limestone bedrock with a paltry patch of seaweed wafting lazily from the floor. Dimly lit by a clutch of bioluminescent anemone, it could have been lovely, if not for the fact that the egotistical little growths doubled as eyeless sentries. Always listening, always feeling for forbidden movement.

But there was room to stretch out, at least. Unfurl his tentacles, feel the water rushing through his gills–

"Inmate! No jetting!" A guard-anemone pulsed an angry turquoise from the far wall.

"Sorry, sorry." Glixor lowered his antennae and slackened his jowl flaps. As much as the word 'inmate' grated, he couldn't deny that it was accurate. He flared himself out and slowed to a gentle drift.

"Man you must be starving." Flaxnar hummed. She was waiting by the grotto's feeding hatch, an opening in the long shaft that ran the full depth of the embassy, filled daily with fresh fish. It also had one of those smug red lights, controlling when they were allowed to eat.

"Nah," Glixor burred, floating down next to her. "Just cooped up too long."

Flaxnar subsumed her membranes in sympathy. "Yeah, I feel that."

She'd already been down here for over a year when the security team had dumped him through the grating and into the grotto. Flaxnar was an artist, frustrated at the restrictions the Ulaxan Ambassador had put on access to human art. She'd been caught in a human museum, too absorbed in the beauty and strangeness of their alien creations to realise she'd been spotted. When she'd asked what he was in for, he'd been too embarrassed to say.

Signing up to be a missionary of the 'All Seeing Oogla' had been his only option to get offworld, and it just didn't stack up against an artist protesting draconian government censorship. But, getting busted preaching to the wrong crowd had put him here all the same. The Ambassador had given him two options: stay on Earth and translate movies for her, or get on a ship back to Ulaxa and do your time there.

It hadn't even been a choice.

Glixor's empty stomach growled. Through the hatch's mesh, darting fish were clearly visible, but the little red light remained obstinately red.

"Ugh." Flaxnar trilled, her jowl flaps flaring with frustration. She tried and failed to squeeze a tentacle tip through the mesh. "They are really straining the friendship today."

At the word friendship, Bogart's sardonic smile flickered before his membranes.

"Actually, I have a translation question. While we're waiting."

"Glix. Come on." Flaxnar pulsed her jowl flaps, as if she was sticking her tentacle-tip into a twitchy clam. "Any second, it's gonna pop. Any second."

"And it'll stay open for twenty minutes. Please?" Glixor pleaded.

If she'd been a human, her shoulders would have slumped. "Ugh. Fine."

He swam up and away, keeping a cautious optical membrane on the guard-anemone, and led Flaxnar back to his viewing cavern. At the start of his sentence, in-cavern gatherings had been forbidden. But that had been before the Ambassador had delegated the translation program to Cultural Attache Drablux. Since then, the rules had been significantly relaxed. They could even gather in a cavern after work and watch movies together.

Flaxnar dragged herself out onto the cavern floor. She dried herself off while he reset the tape and prepped his translation overlay.

"Ready?" Glixor asked.

"Oh I guess."

He hit play on the last line, and Bogart's staccato, honking voice melded with the melodious warble of his own.

"Louis, I think this is the beginning of a symmetrically tentacled friendship."

Flaxnar crossed two tentacles in front of her abdomen, and stroked her mandibles with a third. He grinned, but kept quiet. How often had she complained that he'd taken on too many human mannerisms? It was nice to know he wasn't the only one.

"Play it again, Glix."

The tape squealed as he rewound it, the VCR's buttons gave a satisfying, tactile clunk as he worked the controls.

"Louis, I think this is the beginning of a symmetrically tentacled friendship."

Flaxnar's optical membranes glistened, and her mandibles spread into a cheerful smile. "Beautiful. This is the beginning of a *beautiful* friendship."

"Isn't beautiful reserved for, uhhh, you know." Glixor snuck a secretive glance at Flaxnar's delicately mottled tentacles, her colouring accentuated by an emerald green waistband she'd fashioned from a scrap of fabric that had floated down the feeding shaft one day. A friendship could be just as beautiful as an exquisite pair of antennae, he supposed.

He coughed, turned back to his dictaphone, hoping she hadn't noticed how feverishly she made his jowl flaps tremble. The silence lingered, far longer than Bogart would have let it. But he was no Bogart, Glixor knew, and that just made it worse.

"That all?" Flaxnar glanced back towards the water, the grotto, and her waiting lunch.

"Yeah." Glixor cast about for something more to say, eventually landing on the empty video cassette case. "It's worth watching, though. If you get the chance."

"It looks old."

"It is. But it's good."

"Did it make you cry?" Glixor's jowl flaps buzzed, and Flaxnar clapped her tentacles together. "Hah! I knew it! You're such a jellyfish."

"Yeah, well..." Glixor quivered, in a very un-Bogart-like manner.

"Ah, I'm only joking. Let me know when you've finished your dub, and we can all watch it together." She oozed away from the TV and slipped down into the water. "Come on. You go get Craig, and I'll catch us lunch."

With a pulse of his tentacles and a growling stomach, Glixor floated up into Craig's viewing cavern. Unlike Fraxnar, Craig would not reveal what he'd done to get trapped down here, translating movies day in day out with them. And at first glance, his cavern was much the same as their own; a cramped, mouldy hole with a stone recess housing the VCR and the bulging TV, and the rickety little platform that kept the dictaphone and notepaper off the damp floor, just high enough that it forced them to hunch up on their tentacles to reach the mike.

But there were differences too, little personal flourishes. A faded cup from a place called a 'megaplex', whatever that was, that he used to hold his pens, and a plastic figurine of a muscle bound human with its arms raised above its head, holding the dictaphone's mike at a convenient angle. Craig was the kind of Ulaxan that had friends everywhere, even at the embassy. Glixor had a sneaky suspicion that in a past life Craig had been a smuggler.

But that didn't mean he wasn't totally dedicated to his translations. Even though it was lunchtime, Craig held up a tentacle, demanding silence, until he was finished with his scene. Not that Glixor minded. It was a pleasure to listen in on a master.

It was a period piece, by the look of the actress on screen, swallowed by a voluminous dress and teetering wig. She spat her lines with a rapid-fire squeak, unusually piercing for a human, that even Craig struggled to match. Eventually, she was drowned out by the rustling of her own pearls and the camera panned to an exasperated man, sitting in a tall canvas chair and holding a megaphone. Craig hit pause on both the video, and his dub.

"Oogla, I hate musicals." Craig hummed, stretching his tentacles up into the air. He must have been hunched over for hours.

"Hey, you chose it. You could have had that Spielberg movie instead."

Musicals were the worst. Matching the slow drawl of human speech was hard enough, but singing too? An involuntary shiver rippled from his antennae right down to the tips of his tentacles. He didn't envy Craig one bit.

"Eh. It was a kids movie. Besides–" Glixor's stomach growled once more, and Craig's antennae pricked open in response. "Lunchtime, I take it?"

"Flaxnar's already at the hatch. Hey, that's new." Glixor whistled. He'd been about to duck back beneath the water when he spotted a pile of white cloth next to Craig's embassy issued black towel, which was neatly folded. Untouched.

Craig's jowl flaps puffed. "Yeah, it is." He plucked two corners out of the jumble and shook out a large rectangle of fabric.

"Is that..." Glixor's words left him, and Craig beamed, his jowl flaps glowing bright green. It was a towel, just like theirs, except it wasn't. At all. The bottom was printed a deep blue. Water, with a swimmer on the surface and a dead eyed monster rising from the deep. And best of all, in bold letters across the top: JAWS.

"That's so cool! How did you–

Craig's jowl flaps puffed even larger, and he held a tentacle up to his mandibles. However he got these things was his secret. No-one else's. He dropped the towel next to his workstation, as if it was just any old towel, and dragged himself over to the water's edge.

"Come on, I'm starving. Plus, I have news." Craig's optical membranes quivered as he dropped over the edge.

"News?" Glixor burbled as he sunk back into the water. It was cool, and heavy with the scent of... Glixor's tentacles twitched. Decapitated crawfish! The acidic sweetness flushed his gills and drove rational thought completely from his mind. His jowl-flaps went into overdrive and, with a hurried flick of his tentacles, he left Craig dawdling in his wake.

The guard anemone's barked, but Glixor ignored them, his tentacles swirling as he jetted straight for Flaxnar and the craw wriggling frantically in her grip. He ripped it away from her without even stopping to ask, and let out a low, almost human moan as the shell cracked and tender flesh came apart in his mandibles.

"So Glix skipped breakfast again." Craig trilled when he finally caught up, accepting the proffered fish from Flaxnar's outstretched tentacle.

"Mmmphh." Flaxnar swallowed. "Let me guess. *Four Weddings and a Funeral.*"

"Nah. It was *Sleepless in Seattle.*" Craig held the still wriggling fish just below his open maw. Teasing. "He's got a crush on Meg Ryan."

Glixor's jowls flushed a bright purple, and his stomach burbled an emphatic betrayal.

"No way!" Flaxnar giggled.

"I do not! Besides, what about you and Bruce Willis?" Glixor protested, trying not to sound jealous. He clung to the mesh of the feeding shaft and tried not to stare as she plucked the remnants of a fin from the hinge of her left mandible. "You haven't stopped talking about *Die Hard* for weeks!"

"Bruce Willis? No way. He's such a brute. Alan Rickman, on the other tentacle...."

Craig waggled his antennae. "You did always like a bad boy."

"Suave, sophisticated, motivated. What's not to like?"

"Oh I don't know. Fingers, toes. Hair–

"I like hair. It looks so gentle." Glixor interjected. He sometimes wondered what it would be like to have millions of little tentacles sprouting out of his skin, tentacles he couldn't control, that simply flowed wherever the current might take them. Totally free.

"Meg Ryan's hair, maybe. But what about beards? Moustaches? Chest hair? Imagine hair on your tentacles? On your mandibles?" Craig shivered, and his jowl flaps wobbled like a jellyfish. "No thank you. No hair for me."

Glixor slipped a tentacle through the hatch and latched onto a second, unsuspecting craw. He bit down, revelling in the satisfying crunch of shell and cartilage. Perhaps Craig was right.

Humans were very odd. They were always cooking their food, for a start. If he could just get some time with one, he had so many questions. The movies he'd seen back home had made him curious enough to come here. And being stuck beneath the embassy translating them all day just made things worse.

"You still working on Aladdin, Flax?" Craig asked, flushing fish juice from his gills.

"Nah." Flaxnar picked at the corner of her maw with a dainty tentacle tip. "I started *ET* this morning. The little boy just found the alien in his closet."

"Oh?" Craig's jowl flaps, larger and looser than Glixor's due to his age, hummed. "What did it look like?"

Craig had taken an interest in human depictions of aliens ever since he was first asked to dub *Star Wars* and, amongst all the ridiculous, clam-fisted costumes in that bar scene, he'd spotted something that looked a lot like a Jaambalarian. He'd dived down into the grotto that day, trembling like he'd spotted Jaws lurking in the embassy's darker undertows, and asked for the Cultural Attache. Within minutes, Drablux was heaving herself up into Craig's viewing cavern as he pointed out the Jaambalarian sitting right across from Sir Alec Guiness.

Drablux, her optical membranes hidden behind her dark, reflective goggles, had laughed it off, telling Craig not to be so paranoid, that it was just a coincidence. However, a friend told Craig that in the final version that had been sent back home, the bar scene had been cut short and the Jaambalarian had been removed.

"Like a wogglesack, with its arms stuck on with glue." Flaxnar spat a globule of mucus back through the hatch, sending the fish into a frenzy. She clung to the mesh, her hunting tentacles poised, waiting for the perfect moment to strike. "These crazy monkeys have no idea."

"No, they really don't, poor things." Craig bubbled, but then his optical membranes brightened and he laid four tentacles across the front of his sandstone perch. If he'd had eyebrows, they would have been waggling like Groucho Marx. "But I did learn something very interesting this morning. Very interesting indeed."

"Did you now?" Flaxnar said, not really paying attention. Her tentacles snapped out, and emerged from the hatch with two more fish coiled tight. "You want a third, Glix?"

"Yes, please." Glixor accepted it eagerly.

"*Very* interesting, I said."

"Go on then. We're listening." Flaxnar twisted her antennae, *very* sarcastically.

"Look if you don't want to hear–

"I want to hear, Craig." Glixor trilled, a dim memory of Craig mentioning news, back in his cavern, bubbling up through his waning hunger. "Ignore her. She's just jaded because Alan Rickman's unavailable. Tell me."

"Fine." He flushed his gills, mandibles clacking. "You'll appreciate this. So I'm working on *Singin' in the Rain*. You saw it. It's about love, and jealousy, the invention of talkies–

"Talkies?" Glixor interrupted.

"You know, talking movies. Apparently, the first ever movies were silent, and then they figured out how to add sound..." Craig waved a frustrated tentacle. "Anyway, the plot's not important. About half way through the movie, the characters go to this place called a *picture house*."

"A picture house?"

"Yeah. A picture house. You'll never guess what it is."

Glixor scrunched his undertendrils. The phrase was familiar. He should know it! But nothing came. He looked over at Flaxnar, and she shook her head, mandibles fully occupied with chewing. However, she had floated close enough to listen in.

"I didn't think so." Craig's jowl flaps trembled with glee. Glixor leant forward, so far that he slipped off his algae-covered perch.

"Come on, Craig, just spill it already!" Flax hissed.

"Alright, alright." He bowed his head, holding four of his tertiary tentacles up in the water, and his fifth to his chest. "A *picture house* is a building where humans go to watch movies."

"You mean like our viewing caverns? With lots of TVs and VCRs?"

"No, no no. Way cooler than that. It's just one big room, with hundreds of seats. Bigger than the grotto." Craig spread his tentacles wide. "And one giant screen!"

"You mean they all watch the same movie? Together?"

Craig nodded, and as a trio they fell silent. Hundreds of humans, all in the one place, gasping together, laughing together, cheering together. Crying together.

"That would be amazing." Glixor fizzed, the water seeming to pop with his excitement.

"I want to go. So, so bad." Flaxnar nodded, her antennae erect, all her usual cynicism washed away.

"It would be nice, wouldn't it?" A voice squeaked from behind. "But the ambassador would never allow it."

Glixor's antennae went rigid as instinct jetted him across to the wall. He splayed himself as thin as he could, his skin shifting to match the mottled green of the grotto's walls.

Cultural Attache Drablux was floating at the heart of the grotto and, finally, Glixor's thoughts caught up to his body. That pop in the water, the slight wave of pressure. That had been her, folding out of empty water. Her favourite trick, one that only the highest ranking officials had access to. Normally it set his antennae standing on end. Instead, he'd been so wrapped up in the idea of the picture house that it hadn't even registered.

How long had she been there? Listening in?

"Long enough." Drablux grinned.

Glixor's optical membranes bulged. He stared up at her, and his half finished crawfish floated into her waiting, outstretched tentacle. She studied it for a second, then popped it into her maw.

"Lunchtime is over, I'm afraid. Back to work."

"You heard her, inmates! Back to work!" The guard-anemone flashed, nematocysts flaring.

"But, we–

"No no. No buts. You've been turning out excellent work. Can't have you getting complacent." The soft, bioluminescent lighting flashed off the thin collar she wore just above her membranes. The collar that opened doors and marked her as 'The One In Charge'. "So, I suggest you do as the guard-anemones say, and jet to it."

Even as she herded them away from the feeding shaft, the hatch closing, its light blinking red at the wave of one of her gloved tentacles, Glixor stared at that collar. If Craig was to be believed, that was what allowed her to materialise in a cloud of bubbles wherever and whenever she pleased. Within the embassy, and without.

"Not you." Glixor stiffened, his tentacles spasming mid-pulse, feeling the rough texture of Drablux's sucker latch onto his back. "New assignments to collect. Follow me."

Grating after grating flashed green, letting Drablux through with a slow hiss. She swam with a confidence that Glixor knew he could never muster here, not when there were anemone's watching every flick of his tentacles, so he pulsed along meekly in her wake.

They saw much more of Drablux than they ever had the Ambassador, back when the Human-Ulaxan Movie Adaptation iNitiative (HUMAN for short. Glixor submerged his membranes every time someone mentioned it) was under her purview. But still, the Cultural Attache didn't just drop by for fun, and she definitely didn't just escort 'inmates' to the archives on a whim.

He put himself in Bogart's shoes; Sam Spade this time. He squared off his upper tentacles, shrank his abdomen down as low as it could go, as if he was hunching down into a sucker length trench coat, and jutted his mandibles. Bogart entered every situation chin first, and so would he.

But Bogart was smart, too. He didn't cause a ruckus unless a ruckus was called for, and right now, Drablux was leading him somewhere he wanted to go. The archives. It was Glixor's favourite place in the entire embassy. Not a high bar to clear, admittedly, as it was one of only three places he'd actually ever been, but still. If he faded into the background, Drablux accidentally might let something slip.

So Glixor did what any good private detective would do. He started paying attention.

The first thing he noticed was that Drablux had a waterproof satchel curled up in the midst of all her tentacles. It must have been almost empty too, because she held it from the bottom and it was floating upside down. The next thing he noticed, when Drablux flared her tentacles outwards and came to a stop, was that they'd arrived.

The entrance to the archives was little more than a puddle in the corner of a low cave, its sandstone walls painted a stark white. Fluorescent tubes hung from the ceiling in rows, each one aligned with a towering rack of video cassettes. Action, Drama, Comedy, Western. There was even a sinister flickering light over the horror section.

Drablux hauled herself out of the water, gravity dragging her normally buoyant body as flat as a soggy pancake. Glixor allowed himself a quiet smile. It was nice to know that even the Cultural Attache was as powerless before gravity as the rest of them.

A boxy portal stood between the entrance and the archive proper. Drablux oozed through it and the air crackled, the portal zapping the surface water from her skin. Glixor's antennae twitched in anticipation.

His first time through the drying portal had been an... *experience*. At once unnerving and exhilarating, like a thousand tiny tendrils prickling his skin from the inside. He flung out a tentacle and dragged himself forward. There was something about the feeling of dry skin that made him want to get *moving*, like all his life the cool, calm heaviness of water had been holding him back.

The archive's racks were calling him.

Drablux slid the empty, waterproof satchel to him across the carpeted floor. Inside he found a printed, plastic slip. A list. He held it up to the light.

"Two weeks worth," Drablux whistled, a cocky trill in her voice, "and, at the bottom, three blank spaces. Your choice, one for each of you."

"My choice?" Glixor's jowl flaps puffed wildly. "Anything I like?"

"Anything you like." Drablux nodded. "Your last two batches have been excellent. Very well received, within the embassy and back home."

"You watch our dubs up in the shallows?" Glixor asked, and Drablux nodded, fiddling with the latch on her own satchel. "Do you have a favourite?"

"*Die Hard* was very popular. The interns were warbling *yip-py-ki-yay* for weeks."

"Yeah, that's Flaxnar's favourite."

Drablux pulled a pair of cassettes out of her satchel and set them in the returns tray. "What's yours?"

"Flaxnar thinks I'm as squishy as a jellyfish, but I can't go past a good romance."

"Really? Though that shouldn't surprise me, given what you usually translate." Drablux extended her membranes. Her jowl flaps flushed, like she was letting him in on a secret. "Yours are usually my favourite."

"Ohh, uhh..." Glixor couldn't stop his jowls from bulging bright pink. "Actually, I'm translating a movie called *Casablanca* at the moment. If you like a good romance, I'd keep an eye out for that one."

"Alright, I will." Drablux turned away and curled her tentacles around one of the polished chrome hoverdisks, floating in its charging chamber. With a casual flick, she sent it skimming over to him, the fluorescent lights reflecting across its surface, one after the other. It reminded him of the alien ship from *Close Encounters.*

"Bring your choices back here when you're done, and I'll help you scan them out."

Glixor almost fumbled the hoverdisk in his excitement, just catching it before it careened off into the maze of movies sitting in their racks. He wrestled it down and clambered over its smooth surface, suckering it securely beneath his undercentre. It hummed gently, sending a pleasurable vibration right up to his antennae. He popped out the control module and tested the balance. It rocked just a little, and he adjusted his grip, until he was sitting dead centre.

"Just don't tell the ambassador." She cheeped, fumbling with her own hoverdisk, a slight flush still colouring her jowls. "And get moving. I don't have all day."

"Yes, ma'am." Glixor peeped back. He didn't need to be told twice.

Controls in tentacle tip, he raised the hoverdisk a good two thirds of a tentacle above the ground, and his perspective of the archives changed. Where before the racks had loomed impossibly high, mountains with unreachable peaks to a dry, gravity flattened Ulaxan, now they were simply tall. He plucked his satchel and his list from the floor and curled all but four of his tentacles around the disk. He jutted his mandibles and, with his remaining tentacles, he walked.

He started at the top of the list, driving the hover disk higher and higher until he was walking not on the ground but climbing across the top shelves of the action section, spinning from rack to rack like something from *The War of the Worlds*. He suckered onto the spines of *Bloodsport, Face/Off, Hard to Kill,* dropping each one into his satchel, and all the while keeping a membrane trained on the shelves, scanning for a title that demanded he choose it.

He pulsed the hoverdisk higher. The next rack was Romantic Comedies. There were two on his list and he could jump right over–

"Hey, watch it!"

Glixor cringed, his antennae curling inwards. He'd almost landed on Drablux's head. "Sorry."

"The archivists are very particular about their shelves." Drablux hummed, her gills flaring somewhere between exasperation and... did he detect the hint of a smile? She had a video curled tightly in her tentacle, the spine pressed against her chest so he couldn't see what it was. "Just be careful."

Glixor swallowed, his mandibles clicking sheepishly. He needed to change the subject. "What have you got there?"

"It's, uhh..." Drablux hesitated, her jowl flaps swelling. Reluctantly, she turned the video she was holding outwards, so he could see the title: *Forrest Gump.*

"Ohhh, Tom Hanks! He's one of my favourites!" Glixor grinned, colour rushing back to his jowl flaps. Then, behind her, he spotted a cassette that was on his list. He reached out and suckered onto it.

"Hey, look at that!" He held out the copy of *Splash*, with Tom Hanks prominent on the cover. "We've both got one, I guess. Have you seen *Forrest Gump* before? Is it good?"

"I heard, uhh, no. The *ambassador* heard about it from one of the human diplomats–" Drablux's membranes widened, her jowl flaps taut. "Anyway, she said it was wonderful. It made her cry, apparently, so I thought I'd check it out." She seemed to gather herself, and whipped the video down into her satchel. "To see if it was worth adding to your next batch of assignments."

Glixor tried not to stare at her still purple flaps. *She's nervous, kid,* Bogart drawled from somewhere in the back of his mind. *Hiding something. Why else would she get the jitters about a rec-ommendation from the ambassador? Keep pushing!*

Glixor squirmed. Sure Drablux was behaving a little strangely, but who was he to interrogate the Cultural Attache? *She's just started to warm to you.* His inner inmate piped up, pushing Bogart back. *Hell, she's allowing you to choose three movies of your own, behind the Ambassador's back no less! And this is how you repay her?*

Prudence won. He'd spent too long down in the grotto making do. And then they get a break. A little choice in a choiceless place. He couldn't jeopardise that for Flaxnar and Craig, let alone himself, on the back of a hunch.

"Oh, right. Well in that case, I look forward to seeing it on the list next time."

"We'll see." Drablux chirped. The mention of the ambassador seemed to have squashed the prior friendliness out of her voice. "I suggest you get a wriggle on. Clock's ticking."

Dammit, Glixor. What was that? He dropped down, until his tentacles touched the ground, and wandered through the lower shelves. He thought he'd been doing the right thing. The safe thing, but he felt as if he'd missed an opportunity. Blown a chance to find out something important.

Worse, he still hadn't chosen even one of his three movies. It was hard enough to agree on what to watch between just the three of them, and they only ever had about fifteen cassettes on hand at any one time. Now he had thousands to choose from, and no way to tell if the ones he picked up were even any good!

He wondered how it all worked at those *picture houses*. Hundreds of humans, all gathered together, agreeing to watch the same movie. Did the picture house have an archive just like the embassy? Who chose the movie, and how big did the TV have to be so that everyone could see?

He bet the Ambassador knew. She must get to leave the embassy whenever she wanted. According to Craig, the embassy was in the middle of a human city. The ambassador could be at a *picture house* right now, right above his head, and he would never know it.

Glixor was four isles over, scanning a rack of period dramas, hunting for a movie called *Amadeus*, when he heard Drablux curse. He pushed away from the rack, floated across to the end of the aisle and poked a membrane around the corner.

Drablux, her head buried in her datashell, unlatched herself from her hover disk and slid it back into its charger. She flopped down to the ground and fumbled her satchel.

"For Oogla's sake." she hissed. Gravity had pulled her almost perfectly flat. "Glixor, I have to go. I..." She touched the side of the copper band around the top of her head, and Glixor felt the rumble of the archive grating sliding shut through his tentacle tips. "Don't break anything. I'll send someone to collect you, and escort you back to the translation hub."

The air crackled, folded, and Cultural Attache Drablux twisted. Then she was gone, and Glixor was alone.

"Hello?"

The echo bounced back a fraction of a second later. He giggled, his jowl flaps puffing out so wide they intruded on the edge of his vision. A flick of a tentacle sent him careening back through the shelves, and for a moment he imagined that they were *his* shelves, *his* movies. That he could choose any one he liked. Or any ten he liked, and watch them all right now, one after another.

He zoomed past science fiction, animation, foreign film, cult classics (whatever that meant), not looking for anything, just enjoying the freedom to move through the air without anyone watching, the bright titles flashing by in a kaleidoscope of fire and blood and neon blues–

A phrase leapt from the blur. More than a title. A feeling. Strong enough to steal his breath away.

He flung out a tentacle, latching on to the nearest upright, his momentum so fierce that his suckers lost the hoverdisk, sending it careening off into the shadows.

And none of it mattered, because curled in his tentacle he held a video. No, not just a video. An idea, sculpted from barbed wire, beyond which pine trees grew tall beneath a wide open sky.

Glixor released his suckers one by one, slipping to the ground, and he took in the determined faces of Steve McQueen, James Garner and Charles Bronson.

He'd found his movie.

The Great Escape.

Back in his viewing cavern, Glixor just could not concentrate. *The Great Escape* was on its second run through, and barely a scene had managed to penetrate the thoughts that buzzed in his head. *Maybe we could... if we just managed...*

He kept imagining the picture house. Soft leather seats, low lights. Hundreds of people, totally silent, holding their breaths. No guard anemones, no feeding shaft. No iron grills with their blaring red lights, inescapable reminders that he was trapped here, that it would be years before they'd let him leave.

And even then, it would be to send him back home.

The tape clicked, clunked. The TV fell to black and Glixor pressed rewind. He still had no idea how the escape had gone. How many had gotten away. All he knew was that he had to show Flaxnar and Craig. Because they could do it. He knew they could. They could get out of the embassy. Swim in the open water once more.

They could go to the picture house. Together. Just sit back and enjoy it.

The tape clicked again, clunked again. Glixor pressed play, and settled down with his notes. He was going to watch it this time. Take it all in, and come up with a plan.

Charles Bronson - Danny, the Tunnel King - was just entering the long tunnel beneath Stalag Luft Thirteen, for the final time, when the floor of Glixor's cavern rumbled, sending a slight ripple across the surface of the water.

The grill was sliding open. Finally. Craig and Flaxnar would be here any minute.

He smashed pause, reached for his satchel of video tapes and began setting them up, the same way they always did when new assignments rolled in. Upright, side by side, face out. A veritable line-up. Just like in *A Fish Called Wanda*.

"Hey-o, what have we here?" Craig burbled as he popped out of the water, his tentacles hitting the cavern floor with a wet slap. "How were the archives?"

"Amazing." Glixor tossed him his towel. He spread himself across the floor in front of the videos, not wanting Craig to get a head-start. He had the whole thing planned. "Drablux left me all on my own."

"All on your own?" Craig's antennae sprung out from be-neath the towel. "What did you do?"

"What do you think I did?" Glixor waggled his antennae, the sound of his chrome hoverdisk, clanging off stone walls while he dangled from the rack echoing in his mind. "But that's not even the best bit. She let me pick any movie I wanted."

"Any movie?" Craig's outer membranes flapped. Behind him, the water rippled. "I don't even–

"How many?" Flaxnar interrupted, hauling herself out of the water, squeezing in by Craig's side and snatching the towel from his limp tentacle. There wasn't really enough space on the floor of any of their viewing caverns for all three of them. Normally when they watched a movie, they would float in the water in-stead. However, for distribution, they needed to be dry.

"How many?"

"How many picks did you get?" Flaxnar trilled, subsuming her membranes.

Glixor beamed. "Three. One each." He latched a tentacle onto a crag on his cavern wall and pulled himself sideways, revealing his haul. "Guess which ones."

Craig hummed, pressing his tentacles together in concentration, and Flaxnar dropped the towel with so little care that it landed half in the water. Not that it mattered much. By the end of the day it was always soaked through.

Off to the side, watching them study his array of video cassettes, the wall vibrated in time with his nerves. *No, wait,* Glixor thought, *that's my heart. Racing.* Good thing they weren't in the water, or they'd know he was planning something.

"Hah, I can pick yours straight away." Flaxnar said, plucking a video from the line-up and holding it out so they could both see: *When Harry Met Sally.* "I mean come on."

"Strike one." Glixor burbled, shaking his head. "That was just on the list."

"Damn." Flaxnar deflated, just a little.

"Lucky Glix! But, what's this? Flax, I think I've found yours." Craig collected the far left video, *Robin Hood: Prince of Thieves,* and offered it to her with a sardonic grin. "Alan Rickman makes such a *dashing* antagonist."

"Give it here." Flaxnar snatched the cassette from him, her jowls fizzing purple. "As if yours isn't totally obvious." She lashed out at a cassette with a completely black case, sending it skittering towards him, across the worn cavern floor.

Craig picked it up, turned the case right way up and wiped it clean with a tentacle tip, his mandibles moving as he took in the cover. "Ohhh. I'm going to like this. Check it out: In space, no-one can hear you scream." He glanced up, his membranes misting over. "Glix, you've outdone yourself."

"Wait, what did you choose for yourself?" Flaxnar had flopped over, eyeing the remaining videos with a hint of confusion. She picked a video and Glixor's breath caught in his gills. "This one?"

She held up *Splash*, the rom-com starring Tom Hanks. Normally, it would be perfect, but not today. He shook his head, jowl flaps wobbling. "You'll never guess."

Flaxnar eyed Craig, but he made a valiant attempt at a shrug (though it ended up more like a protracted shiver that only reached the top of his tentacles). So she swivelled back, her membranes partially submerged. "Go on, then. We give up. You're clearly vibrating to tell us, anyway."

Glixor exhaled, his nerves turning the breath into a low whistle. "Well. I was thinking about what you said earlier today, Craig. About the picture house, and how we all wanted to visit one. Just once. And then Drablux had to leave, you know. She just touched her tentacle tip to her headband and 'pop'. She was gone! And I was all on my own..."

Now that he was talking, the words just fell out. He knew his jowl flaps must be almost fluorescent, that his tentacles were waving all over like he was caught in a storm swell, but he didn't care.

"... and then I saw it. It almost jumped off the shelf at me–

"Glix, what are you talking about?" Flaxnar cheeped.

"This! This movie!" He plucked *The Great Escape* out from the array and held it out so they could both see. "It's based on a true story! They were prisoners, just like us. They made it out, and we can too. I know we can."

He stopped, and his words echoed faintly around his cavern. He stared expectantly at his friends, just waiting for them to swell up with excitement, to voice their agreement, chiming in with suggestions of their own, but Flaxnar was studying the back of the casing, and Craig just looked concerned.

"Whoah, Glix. Slow down there a dry second. Are you saying you want to break out of the embassy?"

"Of course! Don't you?"

"I mean..." Craig wavered, membranes turning to the ceiling.

"But you said. We all said!"

"I know what I said, and yeah, I want to go to a picture house one day, all three of us. I'd love nothing more!" Craig tucked his tentacles under his mandibles, as if he wasn't quite sure how to say the next part. "But Glix... I just..." He puffed out his jowls. "Is it even possible?"

"So I've thought about this, and we'd have to get our hands on one of Drablux's headbands, the ones that let her–

"Glix, have you watched this movie?" Flaxnar burred, interrupting his flow.

"What? Of course I have! What do you think I've been doing since I got back from the archives?"

"Have you?" She held the cover up with the back facing towards him, her tentacle tip tapping a small dedication in the upper left corner, so close to his face that he couldn't ignore it. "Read it. Out loud."

Had he watched it? Only three times this afternoon! But he caught the stern look in her membrane and swallowed his indignation. For now.

"This movie is dedicated to 'The Fifty.' Men of courage, duty, and honour, who..." Glixor stopped, the energy in his jowls, in his veins leaching away.

"Keep going." Flaxnar coaxed, not unkindly.

"... men of courage, duty, and honour, who gave their lives for the good of their comrades." He took the video cassette from her and let it fall into his lap.

"I'm sorry, Glix, but this plan of yours is a really bad idea."

Glixor deflated, embarrassment pulling him down until he was flat against the floor. His vision of breaking free of this place, of running, of sitting down in the dark before the silver screen, with his friends at his side, it was all sinking down into the depths. He'd wanted, he'd wished, but he hadn't really thought, at all.

Flaxnar was right. It was a really bad idea.

Glixor translated and dubbed *The Great Escape*, just as he had *Casablanca*, and countless others. They even watched it together one night, before it went back to the archives, though they didn't talk about it afterwards, like they normally would.

He moved onto the next movie. *When Harry Met Sally. Splash. Amadeus. Driving Miss Daisy. An American Tail.*

Flaxnar shared her newfound love for Nicholas Cage (a definite upgrade, in Glixor's opinion). Craig regaled them with frame by frame dissections of *Alien*'s most genius special effects. Before long, Glixor stopped imagining himself as Captain Hilts, stopped pretending Drablux was the camp commandant, that

Craig, with his contacts in the embassy, could be their scrounger and that Flaxnar could be their forger.

But his dream of taking Craig and Flaxnar to the movies, of buying a big box of popcorn, a choctop each and sitting right in the front row didn't fade away completely. It changed. He accepted that it wouldn't happen here. But when he finally got out, went home, having left the embassy and the archive behind, maybe he'd build one.

A picture house, in a cavern, with a grotto of his very own. He'd have to figure out the details, human technology and water didn't usually mix, but he had plenty of time for that. Craig and Flaxnar would help. And then they could visit, any time they liked.

While Glixor dreamed, Craig made the next trip to the archives and returned with something called a poster folded in his satchel, and Flaxnar fashioned them all what humans would have called an armband. A strip of cloth for one of their tentacles, made out of a battered old t-shirt that she'd found floating in the feeding shaft.

It was almost like things had gone back to normal.

"You sit around here and you spin your little webs and you think the whole world revolves around you and your money." Glixor allowed his mandibles to flap, lending his voice a waver to match Jimmy Stewart's. "Well, it doesn't, Mr. Potter. In the whole vast configuration of things, I'd say you were nothing but a scurvy little–

A rumble, just like that of his iron grill, interrupted his flow. Antennae twitching, he pushed back from his dictaphone and dipped two tentacles down into the water. Huh. It actually was the grating, grinding back into the rock, even though his day had barely started. He flopped over the edge and let the water take his weight, *It's a Wonderful Life* still rolling in the background.

"Inmates!" The guard-anemone's shrill bark reverberated up his now open tunnel. "Out here! Now!"

Jowl flaps pulsing with curiosity, Glixor swam down, out into the grotto. And then he stopped, flaring his tentacles into a float just beyond the entrance. A terrifying Ulaxan, hissing and puffing, marred the usually empty space, with Drablux floating some distance behind.

Glixor stared, his tentacles hanging loose. She was twice Drablux's size, and every part of her bulged. Her membranes, her jowls, her abdomen. The tips of her tentacles were clad in gold.

The Ambassador had returned. And she was furious.

Her antennae vibrated with barely contained rage as she twitched from rock to rock, her tentacles swarming in an uneasy, agitated dance. The Ambassador's movements had the same energy that he'd just seen in George Bailey's furious pacing outside Mr Potter's office. Whatever she was doing here, it could not be good. For anyone.

Flaxnar jetted out from the entrance to her viewing cavern a few spans below, only to flare and float, just as he had. Craig was only a second behind.

"What are you squids waiting for!"

The guard-anemone's order jerked him back to his senses, and he allowed himself to sink down until he was level with the Ambassador, just out of reach. The moment he touched down she lurched forward, her optical membranes cast a demonic black by the red light blaring from the grotto's main entryway. She landed, her tentacles curling so tight around her rocky perch that Glixor feared she might crush it, and she flung a video cassette out into the space between them.

"Which of you coral-brained loons translated this... this..." The Ambassador fumbled for words as the cassette twisted and danced in the current, "...this disgusting... radicalist... propaganda!"

The three of them watched, gills clamped shut as the cassette fell in a slow spiral. The title was obscured in the low bioluminescence. It touched the grotto floor and Glixor jumped. Then it settled, lying face up, for all the world to see.

He froze.

Tom Hanks stared back at him. It was *Splash*.

On either side, Flaxnar and Craig kept their membranes fixed on the stony floor. Glixor felt as if he were made of stone.

"Well?" The Ambassador demanded, her tentacles so taut her mottled skin had turned white.

His jowl flaps buzzed an electric purple. There was no point hiding it. With his mandibles clenched tight to prevent them from chittering, Glixor met The Ambassador's seething black membranes and raised a quivering tentacle.

"Ugh." She spat. "At least you're not so guileless as to lie about it, too."

The Ambassador lashed out with two tentacles, lifted the cassette up and crushed it before his eyes. "Drablux, deal with them. I don't want to hear another parched word about Tom bloody Hanks!"

The Ambassador touched a tentacle to the copper band around her head, and twisted away in a burst of bubbles. The shattered remnants of *Splash* danced in the shockwave and sank to the grotto floor amidst a stunned, heavy silence.

Drablux drifted forwards, careful to avoid the sharp plastic shard and twisted coils of magnetic tape.

"For Oogla's sake, Glixor. How could you have missed it? A water-dweller, welcoming a human, a *human*, into our world? You know how they treat their oceans right? Can't you smell it? Every day when the feeding shaft opens? How did you think the people back home would react?"

"I..." Glixor faltered. After all that, how could he say that he'd thought it was just a nice movie? That he hadn't been home for so long that he barely remembered it? How could he know that people would take such a silly story so seriously?

"You know this is worse than *The Little Mermaid* incident, right? At least then we could pass it off as a ridiculous fantasy. I mean a water-dweller, giving up their fins to live on land? Who would believe that! But this?" Drablux fidgeted with a coil of tape, avoiding their gaze, as if she knew what was coming and really didn't want it to. "And it was all going so well."

She tossed the tape aside and unfolded a slip of plastic. She read from it without looking up.

"The Ambassador has made some changes. You'll now have strict content guidelines. Anything that comes within a hundred tentacle spans of those guidelines is to be reported and all translation works halted." She swallowed. "There will be audits."

"And, there will be no more watching movies together after your work is done for the day. In fact, there will be no more gathering in the viewing caverns at all." Flaxnar gasped, and Drablux's jowl flaps turned sallow and concave. "The gratings will open four times a day, for one minute only each time. To let you in, to let you out and back in for lunch, and then out again when your work is done. At all other times the viewing caverns will be off limits."

She raised a tentacle tip to the band at her forehead and, finally, met Glixor's gaze. "For what it's worth, I think she's going too far. I tried to talk her down, but to be frank, we're lucky the program is being allowed to continue at all."

Then, with a touch of her tentacle, the water fizzed, popped, folded, and Drablux was gone.

Glixor floated loose from his perch, mandibles slack and antennae stunned straight. He couldn't take his membranes off the curls of tape twisting up into the water.

"They can't do this!" Craig hissed, out into the grotto. "They can't do this, right?"

As if in answer, the grotto rumbled. Their grates were opening.

"You heard the woman! You've got one minute!" The guard-anemone's shouted, their nematocysts pulsing a power hungry orange. "And don't go getting your tentacles caught. Those grates won't wait for nobody."

"But she can't!" Craig jetted up to the guard-anemone, his jowl flaps taut with anger. "How are we meant to translate if we can't talk to one another–

"We don't care how, and neither does she." The guard anemone's bristled, bright red and yellow. "Thirty seconds!"

Glixor watched Craig's protestations with a numb resignation. There was no point arguing. The Ambassador had total control over their lives. He flailed his tentacles, and barely moved.

No more movie nights. No more debates about the meaning of a certain word or a perplexing body movement, no more laughter at the pure absurdity of humanity's ideas about what life might be like elsewhere. Nothing but work, food and sleep.

Drablux hadn't said it, but that's what she'd meant. Even out of the water, he'd never felt so heavy in his life. Flaxnar jetted towards him, trying desperately to catch his gaze, but he rolled away, drifting listlessly towards his viewing cavern.

There was nothing else to do.

Glixor oozed back to his workstation, not even bothering to dry himself off. Out of the water, gravity squeezed his body to the floor. He unfurled a tentacle, letting it roll towards the remote. He was relieved when it didn't reach. The thought of watching George Bailey's confected descent into depression, or the saccharine revival triggered by that bumbling angel, made him feel ill.

He and Flaxnar and Craig, they had no angels coming to their rescue. No. *It's A Wonderful Life* was not what he needed right now. With a half-hearted flop, he rolled across to his stack of video cassettes and cursed. *The Princess Bride. Big. Ferris Bueller's Day Off.* A collection of feel good tosh. Totally useless.

Glixor needed Bogart. A man who knew how to take punches and bide his time, who worked within the confines of the system when he had to, and then broke the rules when his conscience demanded it. He needed *Casablanca*. The casing may have gone back to the archive, but the cassette itself had stayed. He'd kept it in the hollow behind his TV, warm and dry and safe, just in case.

He reached a tentacle into the cavity, the boxy TV humming slightly and the screen tickling his skin with static–

Glixor's breath caught. His tentacle tip had landed on not one video, but two.

He threw a wary glance back at the still surface of the water. It glowed a dull red. He was still alone. His tentacle probed and confirmed: two sets of reels, two spring loaded lids. He ran a sucker along the title block, yet all he sensed was paper and ink. As sensitive as an Ulaxan's suckers were, he couldn't read with them.

Had he put a second video there? No. He was certain. There should only be one, and yet there were two. Curiosity burned through the fog. He curled his tentacle, scooped both cassettes up, and peered into the shadows.

There they were. Two dusty black rectangles, clear plastic windows through which the magnetic tape was visible, both wound back to the start. *Hah!* Glixor thought. *At least whoever put this tape behind my TV was considerate enough to rewind it for me.*

His jowl flaps bulged, sending pulsing shivers up to his gills and down to the depths of his undercentre. The top cassette he knew. It was Casablanca. Even with his tentacle wrapped around it, he recognised the title block. But the second...

He exhaled. Closed his optical membranes, unaccountably nervous. It could be anything. *Great Expectations. Monsieur Hulot's Holiday.* Absolutely anything. It wasn't necessarily a sign, or an omen. Whatever it was, he shouldn't read anything into it.

He opened his membranes and he wheezed, the air fleeing his lungs as if it was just as much a prisoner as he. His tentacle went limp, and the cassette clattered to the ground, landing title block up. He stared.

The Great Escape stared back.

The hours until lunch crawled by slower than a Coral Slug after a Kingtide Dinner. Once again Hilts and Danny were strutting across his screen and Glixor wasn't even watching, too preoccupied with lunch and what he would say when he saw his friends.

Craig. It had to have been Craig. No-one else knew of his hiding spot. But why? They'd all agreed it was a bad idea, that his plan had been ill-conceived at best, terrible at worst. The minutes dragged, without a hint of respect for his agitation.

When the red light turned green and the rumble finally came, Glixor was already in the water. He squeezed through the gap before it was wide enough, scraping his jowls on the rock and not caring one bit. He dove out into the grotto and circled the cavern, restless, waiting for his friends. Where were they?

"They're not coming, inmate!" The guard anemone's croaked, once again seeming to read Glixor's mind. "Lunch is now staggered. You have ten minutes."

"How are we meant to–" Glixor stammered.

"Ten minutes, inmate, and you're lucky to have that if you ask us." The anemone's rippled bright orange.

"I didn't ask you." Glixor flared his jowls, his mind churning. His stomach growled as the scent of fish hit him, and his boiling anger turned ravenous.

"You better watch your mandibles–

"Or what? What can you do? Wobble those little polyps you call tentacles? Shout at me some more?" He splayed his jowls and he glared at the anemones. A half-dozen new guards waved back, totally unintimidated. Where had they come from?

"We can do this." The anemone's snarled, their nematocysts coiling with menace. They pulsed, and the feeding hatch snapped shut.

"Hey!" Glixor howled, diving down and clamping his suckers onto the hatch's surface. He tugged and pulled with everything he had, but the hatch remained resolutely closed. Its red light attracted the fish that should have been his lunch, close enough to catch but just beyond reach.

"Looks like lunch is canceled. Unlucky." The anemone's relaxed, letting themselves sway in the current as if they didn't have a care in the world. "Five minutes."

Glixor hauled at the hatch one last time, but it was no use. *Well done, idiot.* All he'd done was make things worse. He jetted away, back towards his cavern, using the rushing water to drown everything else out. If he couldn't eat, at least he could stretch his tentacles, and think.

He circled past the entrance to his cavern, past Craig's, past Flaxnar's, careful to keep his speed just this side of the line. The grotto might have been larger than his cavern, but within thirty seconds he was back again. And again. There must be a way he could get a message to them. Of course, they could talk at the end of the day, but the anemone would be there. They were always there. Observing.

He rounded the grotto, swimming aimlessly. All that mattered was the water flowing over his body, between his tentacles, through his gills. He wove around rocks, under ledges and over outcrops. Then, a flash of white.

By the time it registered he was past it. Something protruded from the gap between Flaxnar's grating and the wall. Something that shouldn't be there.

"Thirty seconds, inmate."

He sucked in his jowls and held his breath. He had one more pass. He skimmed the wall so close his wake reflected behind him, rippling his trailing tentacles. Mandibles open, membranes trained on the fleck of white. Three. Two. One...

He clamped his mandibles shut, catching it, ripping it free. By the time he'd flared his tentacles and rolled past the slowly opening grating to his viewing cavern, whatever it was was secreted in one of his jowls.

Flopping out of the water, he coughed the white something out onto the ground. It was paper, folded tight. With two tentacles he pried it open and spread it flat. On the very inner fold, where it would be most protected, there was writing. The ink had run, was still running, but it was legible. Just.

We have to get out of here, it said. *But we need a plan.*

By the end of the day, Glixor's empty stomach had taken almost total control of his senses. He couldn't stand being in the water. Even hours after lunch he could smell the remnants of Flaxnar and Craig's meals, seeping into his skin. Teasing him, and drawing him down to the closed grating and the blaring red light. He just couldn't take it.

Instead, he'd remained dry-side, and distracted himself with *The Great Escape.* He filled his notebook with scrawled thoughts, half-baked tactics and impossible plans. Nothing solid though.

Nothing usable. Finally the grating rumbled, and, his mind still fuzzy with unresolved possibilities, Glixor rolled towards the grotto.

He dangled his tentacles into the water and let himself slide over the edge. It all came back to the tunnel. The humans had shovels and nice soft dirt. What did they have? A few video cassettes, a TV, Craig's posters and solid stone walls. They may as well have had nothing–

Water flushed through his gills: sweet traces of tender, juicy flounder flooding his senses. His stomach roared, and all thought ceased.

The scent drew him out of his cavern, pulling him as if he'd been hooked by the mouth. It was more than just remnants of long ago lunches. In his heightened state, he tasted familiar algaes and planktons. Traces of acidity, of rot, of alien places and alien lives. All of it pouring from the open hatch in the feeding shaft...

The feeding shaft.

Maybe they didn't have to dig at all.

Careening through the water, he fought to regain control of his body, to push his hunger to one side. He had to get a look inside. Perhaps he could catch two trout with one hook?

He gave in to his hunger and slammed into the rock beside the open hatch. Good. The guard anemone's would see it and smirk. He was frantic, not thinking straight. He leaned into the frenzy, rammed three tentacles and half his head through the open hatch, desperate for a fish.

He looked up.

The shaft yawned away from him, up and up and up. Patches of light wafted through open hatches, darting fish sparkling then flicking back to shadowed arrows. A current dragged at him, just slightly, sucking his tentacles down. Way up, right at the edges of his vision, something whirled. The vibration travelled all the way down the shaft, a soft *whump... whump... whump.*

An impeller.

Black fins against an alien light.

Yelling behind him. Suckers on his back. A fish glanced off his forehead and his hunger reasserted control. Instinct flashed his tentacles out and they curled once, twice, three times. His jowl flaps flushed purple, absolutely buzzing, as he was wrenched back into the grotto.

"Merciful Oogla, Glix! You skip lunch or something?" Craig laughed, though Glixor could barely hear him over fishbone's crunching and the guard anemone's shouting. He offered a sheepish nod.

"Your friend here has a smart mouth, so we skipped lunch for him!" The anemone growled. "And if he's not careful–

"Alright, alright. He's learned his lesson." Craig burbled, holding up his front tentacles in an effort to mollify the anemones, who were vibrating a vengeful purple. He guiding Glixor away from the hatch. "Haven't you, Glix?"

Glix nodded once more, and started in on his second fish. Because he was hungry, yes, but also because filling his mandibles with more fish was the only way he could stop himself from blurting out what he'd discovered.

"Any chance you're going to share?" Flaxnar asked, pulling herself along the grotto floor towards the hatch as if she already knew the answer.

"Mhm-mhm." Glixor mumbled, clutching his last fish to his undercentre and settling around his favourite outcrop.

Craig's jowl flaps pulsed with concern. "Are you alright?"

Glixor wasn't listening. Fish guts drifted in the water, his mandibles mashing and tearing. He was watching the anemones. Bright colours, wafting lazily in the current. He didn't believe it. A burp rumbled up from his stomach and he let it ring out, bubbles trickling along his jowl ridge and up over his antennae.

And the anemones tracked the bubbles, all the way up until they disappeared into the murk, their tendrils curling up as far as they could go. Glixor flicked a bone from the inside of his jowl. There was nothing lazy or random about their nematocysts at all.

"Glix?"

"You know how in *The Conversation*, Gene Hackman turns on the radio whenever he doesn't want to be..." Glixor waggled his antennae at the anemones. "...you know?"

"Ah, yeah?" Craig looked confused, but only for a second. "Yeah, yeah I know it. Good movie. Relevant, you might say."

"Mmmm." Glixor nodded, with what he hoped was a significant air.

"You two are such idiots." Flaxnar burbled, barging in between them to hand Craig a small trout. "What did you do to piss the limpets off, anyway?"

"Not much." Glixor shrugged. "I just pointed out the relative inadequacy of their tentacles." With a casual grin, he bit the head off his last fish.

Flaxnar whistled a laugh. "Well. After what they pulled today, I'm not surprised. And all over bloody *Splash*, too."

"What's wrong with *Splash*?" Glixor asked. "I thought it was rather sweet."

"Oh of course *you* liked it." Flaxnar huffed, sinking down onto her usual rock and tearing the head from her Red Snapper. "Craig, back me up here."

"Yeah, sorry Glix. It wasn't great. Definitely not worth all of this anyway!" Craig raised his voice, making sure the anemones could hear. He paused for a second, then dropped the tentacle that held the still wriggling trout to the ground. "Damn. You know what I just realised? *Splash* might be the last movie we ever argue over. What a depressing thought."

Glixor caught Flaxnar's membrane, and he wondered if they were thinking the same thing. Yes, there it was, a conspiratorial tremor in her jowls. *Just wait until she hears about the shaft!* Glixor thought. He swallowed, and wiped his bloody tentacle on his outcrop.

"Well. We could always pull a... *Steve McQueen.*"

Flaxnar grinned. "You found it, then?"

"I sure did, wait, that was you?" Glixor glanced from Flaxnar to Craig and back again. "I was sure it was..."

"What, Craig? Hah, no way. You would never be so rebellious, would you?"

Craig submerged his membranes, and focused on his dinner. "I honestly have no idea what the two of you are on about."

"What Glix is saying, Craig, is that we might consider doing as Ellen Ripley did, you know? Snake Pliskin?" Flaxnar's antennae thrummed, and Glixor knew just how she felt. They were creating their own secret language, a code only they could understand, cobbled on the fly. Bogart would be proud. "Andy Dufresne?"

Craig's optical membranes went wide, and his mandibles curled into an 'O'. "But you said it was a terrible idea. It *is* a terrible idea!"

"Yeah, Glix's plan was awful." Flaxnar shrugged. "But it got me thinking. And then..."

She left her sentence floating in the water, and turned her membranes towards the angry red lights that barred the entrance to their viewing caverns, the now closed hatch, and the main entrance to the grotto. *Flax probably thinks it's the only way out.* Glixor beamed, his jowl flaps glowing.

"I've been thinking too. The Fifty had an entire camp full of manpower, and Andy Dufresne had twenty to life. We don't have either of those. But, I don't think we need them." Glixor glanced meaningfully across at the feeding shaft, but neither of his friends followed his gaze. Flaxnar seemed confused, and Craig nervous. His membranes kept flicking across to the closest anemone.

"Glix, I'm not sure we should be–

Glixor interrupted him. "Just listen, okay? Every lunchtime, that hatch opens. What do you smell?" He leaned towards Flaxnar, willing her to get it. Fish, purifiers, the scents of a bustling embassy, hard at work. But mixed in with all that, intermingled, was something foreign. Their membranes locked, and her mandibles spread into an eager grin. She'd smelled it too. Something exotic. Something human.

"Glix, you're absolutely brilliant." Flaxnar squealed, glancing up at the mass of the embassy that sat above their heads, her jowl flaps fizzing with excitement.

"I..." Craig crossed his tentacles across his abdomen. "If you two are going to keep having half conversations then I might as well–

"Oh for Oogla's sake, Craig. Take a shaft and turn it sideways, what do you get?" Flaxnar snapped.

"I dunno, a tunnel I guess? But I don't..." Flaxnar bulged her membranes at him, jutted her mandibles, and for the second time in a minute Craig trailed off into silence.

"Yeah. Like I said. Brilliant."

"Maybe." Craig twisted on his rock, taking in the feeding shaft, the tiny hatch. "Your McQueen, though. Andy Dufresne, they didn't just, you know. They had plans. For after." He turned back around, holding up his tentacles, suckers out, his jowl flaps sunken with worry. "And they were human!"

Glixor opened his mandibles, but nothing came out. Instead, *The Great Escape* replayed itself in the back of his mind, every scene cast in a new light. They didn't just dig tunnels. They forged documents, scrounged supplies, made disguises. It wasn't enough to get past the fence. Even Hilts' first aborted escape had been in service of refining the plan. All that effort was focused on what happened next.

But Germans, Brits, Americans, they were all human. They all had the same number of arms and legs. All it took for the Fifty to blend in was a uniform and a permit. If he'd learned anything from *The Thing*, from *Alien*, humans did not take kindly to strange looking creatures crawling around their midst.

Glixor turned to Flaxnar, his hope leaching into the tepid water. She sat perched on her rock like a coiled spring, and her eager grin hadn't faded one bit.

"Well, while Glix has been thinking with his stomach, I've been thinking with my head. I showed you *ET*, right?"

"Yeah..."

"And you dubbed *War of the Worlds*, right?" Craig gave her a non-committal shiver. "Did those flying saucers remind you of anything? Anything in, say, the archives?"

Of course! Glixor curled his tentacles with triumph, and it took all of his control to stop himself from jetting up into the water. Genius. Absolute genius. He'd always imagined Flaxnar as their tunnel queen, but that wasn't her at all. He glanced down at the tentacle band she'd made him, a neatly sewn piece of scrap fabric. She wasn't their tunneler. She was their master of disguise.

Meanwhile, Craig was stammering. "You can't mean–

"Yes, Craig. That's exactly what I mean. And if we can figure out a way to stockpile towels–"

"Hang on, hang on. How are we meant to get... I mean they won't even let us watch a movie together!"

"You'll think of something, Craig." Glixor interjected, too excited to remain silent. "You are our scrounger, afterall."

"Scrounger?" A smile crept from Craig's mandibles all the way up to his antennae. "Hah, I suppose I am, aren't I."

Without the anticipation of what was to come, Glixor didn't know how he would have gotten through that next month. The Ambassador's edicts were strict, and the anemone's enforcement merciless. Days were long, and movies blended into one another, their translations and dubbing efforts impeded by a seemingly endless stream of bureaucratic cross checks.

But, squeezed into the margins of day to day existence, preparations were under way. Every lunchtime, Glixor scouted the feeding hatch, confirming dimensions, and every evening Flaxnar made he and Craig prance about the grotto floor as if they were walking on their tentacle tips, taking measurements and assessing fit, form, and function in her head.

The archives, though, turned out to be the key. Because of the Jaambalarian incident, Craig was the only one the Ambassador trusted. Without his weekly trip into the belly of the embassy, their plan would have gone absolutely nowhere.

That first week, Craig returned to the grotto with a satchel stuffed full of videos, and was granted special leave to visit each viewing cavern, for two minutes each, in order to drop off new assignments. He burst from the water and tipped a pile of cassette tapes onto the floor, shoving five at random into Glixor's waiting tentacles and accepting a towel in return. A week later, according to Craig's telling that night, Flaxnar had crammed three finished disguises in with the remaining videos, which made their way across to his cavern to join their growing stash of supplies.

Week three brought a rushed sketch of the embassy and a tattered map of a town called Miami Beach. Unfolding the map with the utmost care, Glixor didn't even notice that Craig had gone, leaving only a stack of new movies beside his TV.

Glixor reached up into the recess behind his mandibles and probed his mucous gland, just as Craig had done with his posters. Four dabs later, the blueprint and the map were hanging from his wall. As he studied them, he idly, almost mindlessly, flipped through his new assignments: *The Breakfast Club*, *Raging Bull*, *Scarface*, *Predator*–

He grabbed for *Scarface* again and read from the back. *Al Pacino... Tony Montana... on the sun-washed avenues of Miami...*

He rammed it into the video player and pressed play, keeping a membrane out for landmarks he might be able to align with his map. The movie washed over him, hot sun and white powder, ambition and violence. By the time the credits rolled, Glixor had half a dozen buildings marked on his map, and a mental picture of what he faced.

If he'd needed any more convincing, *Scarface* was proof. Luck was with them.

By week four, they would be ready.

Today was the day.

Craig had made his last visit to the archives, and emerged from the water with a satchel filled not with video cassettes but with everything they needed for their escape. All he needed now was the map. With jowl flaps trembling, Glixor pulled it down and folded them away.

"No trouble with..." Glixor asked.

"Nothing major. One was already missing. What do three more matter?" Craig shrugged. "You ready?"

Glixor patted his TV antenna, unplugged and ready by the water. He looked Craig in the membranes and stilled his shaking jowls. "Yeah. I'm ready. We're ready."

"You better believe it." Craig wheezed, his mandibles flaring into a nervous smile. "When the light goes green."

Glixor nodded. "When the light goes green."

With hours to kill, Glixor should have been watching *Scarface*, making a final check of his landmarks, or *The Great Escape*, searching for one last crucial insight. Instead, he slid *Casablanca* into his VCR, and imagined he was as brave as Humphrey Bogart.

Glixor clung to the algae slick rock, just inside his grating. Secreted between two tentacles, he held his TV's antenna. Ready and waiting.

He tapped the metal, just once, and felt the answering taps, first Flaxnar's then Craig's, through the suckers pressed against the crusting iron.

Optical membranes trained on that implacable red light, he tried to put himself in his friends' suckers. Craig would be nervous, his antennae vibrating so fiercely that the anemone would be able to sense it through the grating. He was probably clinging to the wall too, thinking that if he'd folded the disguises slightly more efficiently, he could have squeezed his posters into the satchel he curled tightly beneath his undercentre. Just for safe-keeping, of course.

Flaxnar, on the other antennae, would be jetting back and forth, unable to hang still. Her hundreds of hours absorbing the best of Schwarzenegger and Van Damme, Stallone and Segal, would be pumping her adrenaline to the limit, making every second crawl by, desperate for the action to start.

Not long now, Flax.

Glixor adjusted his grip on the thin antenna tube, and rehearsed his movements with half closed membranes. When the first rumble of the grating sliding back reached his suckers, it didn't register.

Then, as the vibrations travelled along his tentacles and up through his body, he froze. There were so many things that could go wrong. What if's swirled, but he leaned into the grinding of iron against rock, using the low thrum to beat them back. Yes, things would go wrong, but they would adapt. This wasn't a prison camp, and Cultural Attache Drablux wasn't a Nazi.

And he wasn't Humphrey Bogart. But he didn't need to be.

He drew a long slow pull of water through his gills, released his suckers and swam out into the grotto.

The feeding hatch was open, its light bright green. He aimed for it and pulsed down, quickly, but not alarmingly so, as if he was hungry after a long afternoon's work. Concealing the antenna stiffened his usually graceful curl through the water, and he felt horribly conspicuous. He rolled as casually as possible, keeping the metal as far from the probing senses of the guard-anemones as he could.

"You hungry, Glix? I'm starved." Flaxnar sang the coded message from the opening to her viewing cavern. *All clear?*

"Me too." Glix warbled back. He was almost there. *All clear.*

"Me three." Craig whistled. "I'll be down in a sec. Catch me something." *Ready and waiting for your signal.* Craig sounded tense, his voice thin and tight.

Glixor flared and put his body between the hatch and the guard-anemones. With four tentacles, working furiously, he rammed the dual prongs of the TV antenna into the opening and braced them against the hatch's bottom lip.

"Trout, Craig?" *Go! Go! Go!*

A moment of silence. Then:

"Hey! No jetting–

Glixor pulled back. A long purple shape shot past him, right through the opening. A second behind, Craig flared out and, in a panic, shoved the bulging satchel away from him. Two tentacles snatched it through.

"What are you doing–

Their membranes met. Craig's jowl flaps jumped and skittered in an arrhythmic pattern, and his mandibles hung open. Without any momentum, he was sinking down, away from the hatch. The green light flared red, and the hatch juddered and strained against the bowed antenna.

Glixor lunged.

"Come on!" He squealed.

The guard anemone's bleated warnings and alerts, the whole grotto echoing with alarm. Glixor wrapped two tentacles around Craig's abdomen, thrust four more through the hatch and pulled. Water rushed, flesh rasped against harsh metal edges. Craig babbled, whistling in protest.

With a sharp twang, the antenna snapped and the feeding shaft twisted, spun, went dark.

A panicked trout slapped him in the jowl with its tail.

"What took you so long?" Flaxnar hissed. She had the satchel, and was already a dozen spans above them. "Get a wriggle on!"

Glixor swivelled, and Craig was spread flat against the shaft wall, his jowl flaps completely drained of colour. Then he grinned. "We're really doing this."

"Yeah. We really are." Glixor, drifting down in the gentle, impeller induced current, held out a tentacle. "Let's blow this joint."

Craig took it, peeled his suckers from the wall and jetted up after Flaxnar. Glixor floated for a second longer, sparing one last look for the inside of the hatch and his mangled TV antenna.

Step one. Check. His mandibles chittered.

With a long, graceful pulse of his tentacles, he raced up the shaft after his friends.

"I don't know who drew you that map, Craig..." Glixor trailed off as he squinted into an oily darkness. Water gushed from a large hole in the wall of their metal tank, churning the surface of the water and smelling faintly of chemicals. The only light came from the shaft below, casting flickering, moving shadows through the slow rotation of the impeller.

This was not what he'd been expecting.

"You said the feeding shaft went all the way to the surface." Flaxnar hissed, barely audible over the crash of the water.

"It does!" Glixor could hear the panic in Craig's voice. "Gimme that satchel and I'll–

"Oh so this dank, slimy box is actually the outside world. What a relief!"

"Quiet you two. Look at this." Glixor whistled. He let the gushing water drift him across to the wall opposite the opening. A metal frame clung, dropping all the way below the surface. "I've seen one of these before. They had them in *The Great Escape*, in their tunnels. They used them to climb down from the surface. I think they're called ladders."

He threw a tentacle up onto the highest rung he could reach, then a second, and pulled. Water sloshed off his back and gravity elongated his body. He threw another pair of tentacles at the next rung up and heaved again.

"I think I can see the top!"

The metal was cold against his suckers. It smelled old. Degraded. He discovered it was easier to work in threes: three tentacles across three rungs. He learned the rhythm: grab, pull, release. Grab, pull, release. Grab, pull–

"Glixor!" Craig hissed. "Listen!"

"What?" Glixor hissed back, but in the momentary silence between pulls, he heard it.

Footsteps, echoing across... wherever they were. Heavy, human footsteps.

He peered up at the top of the ladder. Evenly spaced, vertical metal tubes ringed the tank, and they were all connected at the top by a long, horizontal rail. A handrail! And footsteps!

"Guys, you know what this means?" Glixor trumpeted, leaning out over the water. "We made it out. We're in the human world now!"

"Yeah, and there's a human coming right for us!" Craig squeaked. "Get down, before they see you!"

But Glixor didn't get down. Not when he was so close to freedom. Instead, he took a deep breath and pulled. Even from halfway, he could tell that the handrails would tower over him. And if they were built for a human–

With a great clang, a white plastic tub twice the size of his TV crashed down on top of the handrail, right above Glixor's head. Two gloved hands gripped it, one on either side, and heaved.

"Glixor, watch out!" Flaxnar squealed, but it was too late.

The tub tipped over, and a silver slurry of ice and fish cascaded down. He curled his tentacles tight, pressed his body flat against the rails and held on for dear life. Fins, spikes and frigid shards battered down on him, breaking one tentacle away, then two. But then it was over.

Below him, the surface of the water churned and settled. Above, the white tub clattered to the metal floor and the footsteps faded away.

"Glixor, are you okay?"

Glixor shook his head, a shiver travelling from his antennae down to the tips of his tentacles. "Did you guys see that? That human has been feeding us this entire time!"

"We're fine too, thanks for asking." Craig trilled. "Wait, Flax, where are you going?"

"Up there. Before the human comes back."

The vibration of Flaxnar latching onto the bottom rung hummed up the ladder as Glixor pulled his way to the top. He flopped over onto a metal grating, almost exactly like the grill that blocked the entrance to his viewing cavern, except it was flat.

"Flax, check it out!" Glixor pressed his tentacle tips into the metal and mottled his skin a wet grey, until they matched the familiar cross-hatched pattern. "Just like the t1000!"

"What?" Flaxnar oozed over to the top of the ladder and peered back over the edge.

"Robert Patrick? In Terminator 2?" Glixor peeled his tentacles away, letting his skin fade back to normal. "You know, after he gets sprayed with the liquid nitrogen and starts to malfunction–

"Okay, Glix, that's very cool. But can you help, please?"

His grin faltered, but only a little. He skidded across the grating and went sucker to sucker with one of Craig's flailing tentacles. He curled two more around the far handrail and hauled Craig, and the satchel, up onto the walkway.

"By Oogla's mandibles, that was unpleasant." Craig coughed, scanning the walkway for any sign of the human. Glixor could still hear his footsteps, and the faint sound of someone whistling, but that was all. They were alone.

Craig waggled his antennae over Flaxnar's shoulder. "I take it we're headed that way?"

"Why do you say that... ohhh." Glixor followed Craig's gaze. Behind Flaxnar, beyond a maze of walkways and gantries, a soft yellow light sparkled off the water, casting effervescent ripples across the low brick ceiling. On the far side of this man-made cavern, a low tunnel burned with light.

Sunlight.

"Looks like a bit of a long swim. Wait, what would a human say?" Flaxnar pulled herself up on the lower beam of the handrail to improve her view. "Walk? Hike?"

"Hike, I think." Craig nodded. "And we'd better get moving, before–

Copy, Jose?

Static crackled overhead, an electric echo. Glixor's gills clamped down and he oozed flat, his skin shifting back into the grey mottle of the walkway grating.

Yeah, go ahead.

Are you anywhere near the upper weir purified water tank?

Sure am. Just finished the 6pm fish run.

You didn't see anything out of the ordinary?

Like what?

Glixor took the momentary break in the radio conversation as an opportunity to force his gills open, and to breathe. He'd spread himself so flat he could only see handrails and glistening bricks in the ceiling shadows.

There's a couple of suits on their way out to meet you. Something down there that shouldn't be. Keep an eye out, yeah?

Roger. Any specifics?

What do you think?

Hah, copy that. Jose out.

The radio chatter ended and the walkways fell eerily silent. Glixor pressed himself against the railings feeling for vibrations. For footsteps.

"As I was saying, we'd better get moving. Before *suits* happen." Craig said, peeling himself away from the edge. They'd all watched enough spy movies to know what *suits* meant. "Come on, Glix. You're the one with the map in your head. How do we get out of here?"

Glixor wrapped his tentacles around the nearest upright and pulled himself across the walkway, suckers curled up for minimum grip. He slid all the way to the next ladder along and peered over the edge.

Below him, water shimmered and a slow, stinking trickle dripped from another opening in the far wall. But this tank was different. It wasn't totally enclosed, like theirs was. It was linked with the tanks on either side by low arches. He gripped the top rung of the ladder and lowered himself down. Water, tainted with faded plastic wrappers and mouldering leaves, lapped at the lower rungs.

"You don't seriously expect me to put my head in *that*?" Flaxnar cheeped, her gills scrunched up at the smell.

"You got a better idea?" Glixor stared into the murk, He couldn't see any more walls, but he couldn't see much of anything else either.

"We could–" A metal door opened with a creak so piercing, the hinges mustn't have been greased in over a decade.

"Too late." Glixor grinned. Flaxnar's antennae sagged, and he released his grip on the ladder and plunged down into the water.

The instant his mandibles hit the surface, countless new smells assaulted his senses. Salty, sour, tangy, zesty, foul, foetid, mangy, furry, and everything in between. He flushed his gills, and adrenaline surged. Without even thinking his tentacles pulsed and he was jetting through the strange and wonderful soup, every pulse bringing a dozen new sensations.

"This is incredible!" He called out. "I've never tasted so many–

–things I never wanted to taste in my life." Flaxnar gagged, her mandibles quivering.

"Quiet, Glix." Craig hummed, his membranes jittering as each new flavour demanded his attention. "I hear footsteps!"

"Oh stop worrying, Craig!" Glixor rolled and dove, jittery and overstimulated. "As if they can even understand us. They're just humans! Can't you just enjoy being fr–"

Then, through the murky, polluted water, an arc of sunlight caught his membrane, drawing him like a beacon. He didn't even finish his question.

"Woah."

Sunsets Glixor had seen before, but not like this. Sunlight rippling a path to the horizon, yes. Scudding clouds picked out in the pinks and lilacs of a coral reef, yes. But never the shifting colour and lengthening shadow falling over land. Over sunbleached buildings, swaying palm trees, yachts and cars and windows, sparkling and reflecting in a grand crescendo. And the birds, black darts against a darkening sky.

They floated in the shadow of a wooden boardwalk, great pillars plunging down into the water, encrusted with weed and barnacles. Hundreds of footsteps thundered over their heads, and even they were a mere rumble beneath the cacophony of laughter and conversation, car engines, music and sirens.

It was incredible. It was enticing. It made the grotto seem small, comforting, and safe.

It was too late to turn back.

Flaxnar recovered first. "We should follow the coastline, find somewhere less exposed, where we can get changed."

She spoke quietly, as if there might be someone listening in the chaos. They'd been processing the overload for so long the sun had disappeared, making a silhouette of the buildings across the bay. They had the cover of dusk, but still enough light to see. It was the perfect time.

The boardwalk gave way to a Marina, then a long, concrete promenade. The surface water tinged with a sharp, burning slick that irritated Glixor's skin. They were exposed. Diving down, they jetted along the margins, dodging between swaying weed and twists of rusting metal, until they swam into a region of dark, vibrating murk.

Glixor breached the surface and scanned the horizon, trying to match what he saw to the folded, fading map that had hung from his wall. The purpling sky was obscured by a wide structure overhead. A bridge, bustling with cars. And to his left, a break in the coastline. A canal. His jowl flaps hummed.

"I know where we are. This way."

He brought them to a quiet park, away from the bustle of people. A triangle of trees, rock and bushes where the bridge re-emerged from the sprawl, thrumming with cars crossing the canal. He crept from the water, shaking the slime from his back. Under the cover of a low shrub, noise and light whizzing by just a few spans away but hidden from view, they regrouped.

"Ugh. It's getting everywhere." Flaxnar wheezed, twisting to inspect her rear tentacles, covered in dry leaves.

"I'd forgotten there was so much... everything." Craig said, wiping a tentacle down his back, only managing to collect even more grime on his own suckers. "All this light and noise and rubbish. Look at this!" Craig poked at a faded plastic bottle, caught in the branches of a leafless shrub. "It's everywhere! How do they put up with it? All the time!"

"They're not wet, for a start. We'll feel better when we're dry and covered up." Glixor said, flailing a tentacle, trying and failing to dislodge a garish plastic wrapper. In the end he gave up and just grabbed the satchel. It was time to pass out the disguises that Flaxnar had fashioned from their towels. He shook his out. It was like putting on a uniform. A superhero costume.

"I can't believe we thought this was a good idea." Craig grumbled.

"I bet you weren't thinking that when we saw that sunset." What had Craig expected? They'd all watched the same movies, they knew how weird and wonderful and overwhelming the human world would be. And this was Miami! Even humans thought this place was strange!

"Well yeah, but now it's dark. We're nowhere near where we thought we were, we stink, covered in Oogla knows what. What if we can't get back? We can't survive out here–

"Give it a rest, Craig." Flaxnar snapped. "Try to imagine what it would be like for a human to come visit our world. They wouldn't even be able to breathe."

Another bottle came flying over the trees from a passing car, bouncing off the shrub next to Craig and plonking into the water.

"Lucky them. I'm starting to think the Ambassador had a point." Craig submerged his membranes, his mandibles scrunched up with revulsion. However, he still took his disguise and sullenly shook it out.

Fully extended, the old towels were completely transformed. The fluffy rectangle now had a hood, shoulders, sleeves that ended with fingered gloves, even pockets! And had she... Glixor peered closer. Yes. Flaxnar had picked out the trim with the remnants of that old shirt.

"Flax, these look incredible." He glanced her way long enough to see her jowl flaps flush, then turned his robe side on, searching for the way in. He turned it back again. "Um, how do we put them on?"

"Oh it's super straightforward." Flaxnar burred. "You just–" She raised the robe above her head with two tentacles and slithered four more inside from underneath. With a complicated wiggle, those tentacles slithered up and into the sleeves, simultaneously filling them into arms and pulling the garment down until her head popped out into the hood. "There. You see?"

Glixor saw, and then discovered it was nowhere near as easy as Flaxnar made it look. But, after much grunting and cursing, all three of them were in. He fidgeted with his tentacle tips, pressing them all the way into the fingers of his gloves. He flexed them, and his faux-hand flexed back.

"This is so cool."

"If you check your pockets, there will be two booties, for your walking tentacles. It's probably easier to put them on now." Flaxnar glooped across to the satchel, her movements oddly frictionless now that she was encased in toweling.

"Oh this is much better." Craig grinned, twisting and flexing, testing the limits of his new outfit. "I always wondered why humans wore clothes. They always seemed to cause them so much trouble when they got wet."

"Imagine how much better it will be when you're riding one of these bad boys." Flax whistled as she rolled him one of the three liberated hover disks, its polished surface glistening under the headlights of the passing cars.

Glixor accepted his hover disk with nervous excitement, slid it beneath the trailing hem of his new robe and up into his undercentre. He popped the controller out, worked it down his sleeve and into what he supposed he should call his left hand. He powered it up.

Slowly, gracefully, the hoverdisk pulled away from the ground. With four tentacles pretending to be arms and four more clamping the hoverdisk in place, only two tentacles dangled down beneath his robe. With just his tentacle tips touching the ground, and the hem of his disguise brushing the tops of the loose leaves, Glixor levelled the hoverdisk off. Then, he ventured into his pocket, pulled out his booties and slipped them on.

He was ready to walk.

Glixor took his first tentative steps towards Craig, and thrust out his hand. "Put her there, partner."

With a mischievous grin, Craig matched him, aiming for a shake to make John Wayne proud. However, without fingers or suckers for gripping, the shake turned into a slap that sent Glixor careening off into the bushes, his tentacles scrabbling for purchase on the far away ground.

"Are you two quite finished?" Flaxnar scolded as Glixor extracted himself from the bush, the branches tugging at his robe.

"Sorry, yes. We're done. We're done." Craig lent a tentacled hand and pulled Glixor back upright. He dropped the hoverdisk down by a tentacle width or two. "Lesson learned. Don't have it set so high that you can't recover your footing if you lose balance."

"Better here than out there I suppose. Here, you'll need this." Flaxnar handed him his map, folded neatly into a little square so that it would fit in his pocket.

Glixor squeezed it between his tentacles in one hand, and slapped the map into his other palm. A move he'd seen from so many movies. His jowl flaps fluttered at the novelty of it all.

"Actually, I don't think I do. I know where we are." He tugged the hood down over his antennae, until his face was cast in shadow, and slipped the map into his pocket. "How do I look?"

Flaxnar leaned back, looking him up and down with an appraising eye. She tugged at the shoulder of his right sleeve, adjusted the fit across his abdomen.

"Like a Ulaxan pretending his towel is a robe." She grinned. "You'll fit right in."

"Great. Then let's go." Glixor spun around, careful not to over rotate this time, and started picking his way through the bushes. "The picture house is this way."

Glixor had thought he was ready for the bustling Miami streets. He'd breathed slowly, counting two in and four out, washing his anxiety out with the spent air. This was a world he'd spent years observing. He was steeped in it, up to his antennae.

Then he reached his first set of traffic lights.

He knew what to do. Press the button, wait until the little red man turned green. But there was no little red man. There was a red hand. And a green light right next to it. And a red light next to that, pointing in a slightly different direction. Cars whizzed by at speeds he just couldn't comprehend, trucks so close to the curb that their wind tugged at his robe, sucking him into their wake.

And the people!

They crowded at the crosswalk. Businessmen with neckties and briefcases, women in high heels. Joggers, students, cops, robbers, old men with walking sticks kids, blowing gum, all of them three times his size, towering over him, jostling for position, thrusting knees and hips into his face in their need to be the first one on the road the moment the lights changed.

He'd been worried people would stare. That they'd make fun, or take one look at him and scream. He hadn't expected them to walk through him as if he wasn't even there.

"Glix. Hang back, with us." Craig grabbed him by the hand, pulling him from the throng. They backed up against the wall. "Let's just watch for a second, okay?"

A peal of staccato beeps accompanied the changing lights and the crowd surged, merged with the humans coming the other way, then split apart, like two schools of fish swimming through one another. The lights changed again and the cars, the people, changed direction. Glixor breathed, two in, four out.

This time, they lined up on one side, behind the crowd. Flaxnar in front, Craig in the middle, Glixor at the back. The staccato peal, the changing lights. The surge of people drew them forward. They stuck together, the asphalt and white paint was warm beneath his tentacles, and the humans buffeted him with a careless urgency. The red hand returned, flashing, but he didn't rush. He let the crowd pull him along, and then they were across. They hung back and the crowd left them behind.

After that, Glixor felt they could do anything.

The Miami air was warm and humid, fragrant with the stink of a human city. Salt blew across from the ocean, trash wafted from the alleyways and dumpsters. Human sweat was all around them, and Glixor trod the sidewalk with eyes and mandibles wide.

They found the rhythm in the chaos. Two women in headbands and neon tights, sped towards them and with wheels strapped to their feet. They were moving so fast! But he didn't panic. Glixor shifted left, Craig and Flaxnar skipped right, and the women skated harmlessly by. A dog sniffed furiously in his direction, and the dog's owner yanked on his leash with a muttered apology.

They crossed a second street, then a third, and no-one even came close to knocking him down.

"Flax, does that crowd look different to you?" Glix asked. The fourth corner didn't have lights, and instead of cars the street was lined with towering palms. The crowd didn't gather to cross, but to listen. A man stood on a box with a hat at his feet. He was playing the saxophone.

Craig edged closer, a guileless smile spreading wide in the shadows beneath his hood. "Can you hear that? It's so... warm."

Without the tinny filter of his TV's speakers, the human world was rich with noise: horns and engines, cackled laughter and buzzing flies. And, unlike wetside, where sound was felt more than heard, where ripples and currents muffled and distorted almost everything, the saxophone rose above it all, soft, liquid and crystal clear.

"Glix, Flax. I'm sorry I was such a pain." Craig trilled, swaying with the music on his hoverdisk. "This is the best night of my life."

Craig listened, and Glixor watched. The far corner was dominated by a garishly lit building with curved, multicoloured windows: white stripes picked out with blocks of bold, primary colour. Red, yellow and blue. A sweeping grey sail thrust towards the sky, with vertical lettering.

Lincoln Cinemas.

His jowl flaps hummed and he pointed a gloved tentacle across the way. "Guys. I think we're here."

"Oh wow." Craig leaned back, taking the whole building in. "I guess we just... go inside?"

The entrance was barricaded with swinging doors. Humans approached them with one hand outstretched, pushed them open and stepped right through, letting it swing shut behind.

"Yeah, I suppose so." Glixor pressed against a nearby tree, and braced himself with his bootied 'feet'. It didn't take much force to get his feet sliding across the pavement. "Though opening those doors could be difficult."

"Nah." Flaxnar shrugged, puffing up her abdomen. "Not if you time it right. Watch this."

Without another word, Flaxnar skimmed across the promenade, her diminutive black clad figure locking in behind a human in shorts, a loud floral shirt and a moustache that even Glixor could tell was badly dated. He walked right up to the door, pushed it open and started when he noticed that there was somebody behind him. Glixor grinned as the man stood back and waved Flaxnar through.

Judging from the puzzled look he gave her as she skated past, Flaxnar had whistled her thanks in Ulaxan. But then he shrugged, and disappeared inside. Flaxnar gave them a droopy fingered thumbs up from the other side of the glass.

"That didn't look too hard." Craig said. Glixor could hear his jowl flaps vibrating from inside his hood.

"Yeah, but neither did climbing into these robes. Or crossing the street." He flushed a blast of air through his gills to settle his nerves.

"True, but we managed."

Glixor nodded, and pushed off, scanning the crowd for a likely candidate. There! An elderly woman, all hanging cheeks and tightly curled grey hair, approaching the doors with a walking stick. He hovered back, just far enough that she wouldn't expect him to open the door for her, and darted forward just as she was already walking through.

She gave a surprised start at Glixor's approach and held the door for him, just as the man had for Flaxnar. Cool, dry air sent a chill down his tentacles and he almost lost his footing on the polished tiles, only just catching himself and his momentum in time. As he passed though, he expanded his mandibles in an attempt to lower his voice.

"Thank you, ma'am." He growled, struggling to hold his mandibles in the shape required for the second 'm', so quick after the first.

"At mah age, you should be holdin' the door for me!" The old lady scowled at him and slammed the door closed, the edge swishing past him, missing him by a whisker.

"Argh! Glix!" Craig's desperate whistle was jarring in such a human space. "Help!"

Glixor spun on a clamshell to find Craig splayed at a forty-five degree angle, his robe caught in the door. He scrambled for grip, but every move he made just made it worse. Mottled purple tentacles flashed from beneath his robe, and his hood was falling back revealing terror in his membranes.

"Don't panic, Craig. I've got you." Glixor suppressed the instinct to jet forwards. That would only send him tumbling. Instead, he stepped calmly over, took Craig's hands and held steady, letting his friend right himself.

"Craig! Are you okay?" Flaxnar asked, almost tripping herself over in her rush to help. "I can't believe that woman!"

Craig shrugged his hood back over his membranes and let out a long, shaking breath. "Is it just me, or is it cold in here?"

Glixor glanced furtively around the lobby, worried that everyone would be staring at the strange little aliens who whistled to one another and could barely operate doors, but again, no-one seemed to pay them any attention at all.

"That was too close." Most of the humans seemed to be heading for the escalator, letting it carry them up to the next level. Above it was a sign. "Looks like tickets are up there. How do we..."

"You'll be fine. Just follow me." Flaxnar said. "Come on, Craig."

Glixor took up the rear. Taking that first step onto the escalator, Flaxnar didn't hesitate, even for a second. The moving stairs smelled of scraping metal and hot oil, and rumbled beneath his feet. He reached up to put his tentacle-hand on the handrail just as the other humans did, and clamped his mandibles shut against the excitement. Everything they'd done, everything they'd been building towards, was at the end of this ride.

The top of the concession stand was the first to appear over the escalator's lip: bright lights illuminating advertising hoardings: Popcorn! Choctops! Soda! The walls were clad in a velvet maroon, and the lobby was just brimming with people. He was so entranced by what he saw that when the escalator shoved him off he drifted forwards, his 'feet' trailing along behind, all pretense of 'walking' totally forgotten.

A line of humans snaked up to the counter, and behind it a bright, clear box bubbled with fluffy yellow popcorn. Movie posters lined the walls, cardboard cutouts, even more posters; more than he could count. Actors he recognised, actors he didn't. Every single movie brand new. He didn't know where to–

A tentacle curled around his head, clamped his mandibles and yanked him to one side.

Flaxnar's face loomed large, so close he could count the spots on her gills. She hid behind a cardboard cutout and held a tentacle up to her mandibles, the universal signal for silence. Her jowl flaps flared bright purple. She turned him around, and pointed through a gap in the cardboard.

He followed her tentacle and squinted, seeing nothing out of the ordinary– "Oogbla'v ampemmae!" He mumbled, relieved that Flaxnar's tentacle had his mandibles clamped tight. He flared his gills, and tapped her tentacle, to show that he was back in control. She released him, and he took a deep breath.

"Is that..." he whispered, and Flaxnar nodded. Drablux.

She was dressed much as they were: long robe, fully enclosed sleeves and heavy hood, obscuring her Ulaxan features. If not for the faint shimmer of copper in the recesses of the hood, he never would have recognised her. But now that he saw her, even under a shimmering blue robe that shifted and rippled like water as she moved, her eager stance was unmissable.

"What is she doing here?" He hissed.

"She's looking for us." Craig moaned. "We're done for."

"No, we're not done yet." Flaxnar shook her head. "She doesn't know we're here. If we can sneak back out–

"Wait, look at this." Glixor interrupted, pointing back towards the Cultural Attache, hovering nervously, and the suited human approaching her from behind.

Glixor held his breath. The man was tall, lean, with short cropped hair and dressed in a tailored suit despite the heat. The spitting image of a government suit. He even had polished black shoes that clapped on the well worn carpet. He couldn't decide if they should try to warn her, or hide until he was gone.

Then, the man waved, and Drablux waved back. Glixor leaned forward. The man shrugged off his jacket, rolled up his sleeves. Drablux laughed. Was that, just audible above the burble of the cinema lobby, Drablux's jowl flaps humming?

Glixor turned back to his partners in crime. "Is she on a date?"

"If they are," Flaxnar burred, "That human is way out of his league."

They watched in stunned silence as, hand in hand, Drablux and the human stepped up to the ticket counter. As they bought tickets. As her human lined up at the concession stand and Drablux 'walked' off towards the cinemas. If it wasn't a date, what else could it be? He tracked her across the lobby, past the *Goldeneye* poster, *The Usual Suspects*, *Forrest Gump*–

A bioluminescent bulb flashed in his mind, and Glixor's mandibles fell open. *Forrest Gump!* She hadn't heard about it from the Ambassador. She'd heard about it from him! Her human! *And she hadn't wanted him to know.*

Glixor made a snap decision. "Craig, give me some money."

"What?"

"Hand it over. I'm going to get the tickets." He held his hand out with such certainty that Craig complied without thinking. "You two stay here, wait til Drablux's 'friend' has got his popcorn. We can't risk him spotting you in the line. Unlike everyone else, he'll know what he's looking at."

"Glix, wait–

But Glixor didn't wait. He was already gone.

He propelled himself across the lobby as quickly as he dared, racing to reach the ticket counter before anybody else. His mind whirred, and he grabbed the purple rope to slow himself down as he reached the counter. It was about half a span higher than his head.

He tapped on the glass.

"Can I help you?" A pair of eyes, obscured by a blond fringe, peered down over the edge.

"Yeah, uh, I'm up for a bit of a surprise tonight." Glixor rolled, his jowl flaps fighting to stay wide. He had to keep his voice low, but they just wanted to hum. "Can I have three tickets to whatever the last person bought?"

"Uh, sure. If that's what you want." The till rang, just like it did in the movies. "That'll be... thirteen dollars and twenty cents."

Glixor took the tickets and handed over the money. Three rectangular stubs, with little circles cut out of the corners. *Admit 1: Cinema 4.* He felt he'd never held anything so precious in all his life.

"Hey, kid? You're change?"

"Oh, yeah. Thanks." Glixor coughed, his jowl flaps flushing as his human voice broke. He snatched the coins and darted away.

By the time he got back to the cardboard cutout, Flaxnar and Craig were waiting in line. He hovered and fidgeted, unable to stand still. He clutched the ticket stubs tight in his hands, certain that it was all going to go wrong.

But he knew he had to try. Bogart would.

"Glix, you gotta try this stuff." Craig called out, a bucket of popcorn the size of his abdomen wrapped up in his 'arms'. Under the cover of the cardboard cutout, he inhaled a mouthful and, "Oohmmfmn." His face melted with pleasure.

"You really should." Flaxnar agreed, handing him a tall cup of orange bubbling liquid. "We got a little carried away."

Glixor sniffed the drink, then awkwardly squeezed the straw with his mandibles, trying to create a tight seal. "Thefe were really defigned for humanf, huh." He grinned, sucking. Then his face dissolved as the sugary sweetness exploded in his mouth.

"What do you reckon Drablux is going to see? What are we going to see?" Craig asked, sliding his mandibles back under his hood and stepping out from behind the cutouts, leading the way towards the cinemas.

"I, um, I'm not sure, exactly. I may have panicked, just a little."

"Hah! Well, I guess it doesn't really matter. It's not like we know what any of these movies are anyway."

A teenager in a maroon waistcoat held his hand out, blocking their path. "Tickets please."

Glixor handed them over and watched in horror as the attendant ripped their tickets in two. "Cinema Four, up the escalator and on your left. Enjoy your movie!" The human smiled and dropped one half of the torn tickets in Glixor's outstretched hand.

"But... but..."

"Come on, Glix." Flaxnar whistled, gently dragging him along.

"But he tore them in half! Right in front of us!"

"It must be what they do. He did it to Drablux. He's doing it to the humans behind us right now."

Glixor stared forlornly at the ruined stubs in the palm of his hand before reluctantly depositing them back in his pocket. "It was just a shock, you know? I thought they could be a memento."

He took a sip of his syrup, fit for Oogla herself, and used the moment to steel himself. They were halfway up a second escalator before he realised he was once again riding one of these amazing contraptions. How quickly and easily the incredible became normal, when the mind was on other things.

The escalator spat them out into a carpeted corridor, notable for the close silence in a world that had until now been so entirely full of noise. Three golden signs above three dark doors provided the only lighting: Cinema Six, Cinema Five, Cinema Four. With a reverent air, Glixor led them across the threshold. It was just as he'd imagined.

No. It was better.

A giant silver screen, taller than the grotto and twice as wide filled the entire far wall, protected on either side by heavy red curtains. And then there were the seats. Row upon row upon row, already half filled with families, mums and dads with kids, young couples, old couples, friends in large groups and small. The entire room had a special sort of hush, with soft music seeming to emanate from the walls.

Glixor spotted Drablux's human, his head sticking up above the back of his seat, and he strode forward. He had a job to do–

"What the hell are you doing?" Flaxnar hissed. "She'll see us. Quick, come back, before Craig notices and it puts him in a panic."

Glixor pulled himself free. "You sit at the back if you want. I've got a plan."

"Glix..." Flaxnar's jowl flaps buzzed, and her grip tightened. Two months ago, her touch would have sent him melting to the grotto floor, but he was a different Ulaxan now. Very gently, he pulled away.

"Trust me, Flax. I know what I'm doing."

She nodded, and let him go.

He edged down the row of seats, jowl flaps spasming. Was he doing the right thing? Only three seats separated them. Two seats. It was too late now. Far, far too late.

"Drablux, is that you?" Glixor sang, in his most surprised, upbeat voice.

She snapped around, membranes narrowed with suspicion in the shadows of her hood. Then they widened with shock. "Glixor?"

"What a coincidence, running into you here!"

Drablux's human turned too, and broke out into a wide grin. "Drabbie? Is this one of your colleagues?"

"Hi, yes. I'm Glixor, and this is Flaxnar. We all work together at the embassy." Glixor glanced behind him, back to the entrance. "We've got Craig too, but he's still marvelling at the size of the screen. You'll have to forgive him. He's a bit of a film buff. I think he's in love."

"Sorry, did you say... Craig?" The human asked, his head slightly cocked to one side.

"Hah, yes I did." Glixor laughed. "Don't worry. He gets it a lot. His mum was a bit of a wild child, apparently."

The human's cheeks flushed a slightly darker shade of pink and his smile faltered. "Oh my, where are my manners?" He thrust out his hand. "I'm Fabian. I'm one of Drabbie's counterparts in the Human-Ulaxan Movie Adaptation iNitiative. A pleasure."

Glixor, ready for the handshake, was not prepared for that bloody acronym. However, he steadied himself and returned Fabian's grip.

"Likewise." He trilled, quietly cursing the fabric that stood between him and his first skin to skin contact with a real life human.

The lights dimmed, and an excited hush fell across the cinema.

"Please, sit." Fabian withdrew his hand and gestured down. By his side, Drablux glared. She hadn't uttered a word. "I must compliment you on your accent. Your English is excellent. Where did you learn?"

"From too many movies." Glixor said. "We work on the translating team."

"Is that so?" Fabian's grin suddenly widened. "I don't know if Drabbie's told you yet, but we're working on a joint project. A

Human-Ulaxan co-production." He touched Drablux gently on the foretentacle. "We should get your friends involved!"

"Quiet, Fabian." Drablux burred. "We can talk shop later. This is their first time at the cinema. Let them enjoy it."

The curtains spread wider and, with a flickering hum from up above, light filled the screen. Glixor tweaked the controls on the hover disk and let it lower him down into his seat.

"Keep going." Flaxnar whistled, and Glixor nodded. "I'll go get Craig."

The light and the sound were all encompassing. The bass rumbled his seat, and, even though it was just advertising, he couldn't look away. He took another sip of his drink and leaned back, the sugar cleansing the doubt from his mind. Fabian was on side, and Drablux hadn't immediately dragged them back to the embassy. This just might work.

Flaxnar somehow coaxed Craig down to come sit with them, clutching his popcorn tight. He even managed to give Fabian a friendly, if nervous, wave. Glixor reached across to take his first handful of popcorn, and failed to suppress a groan as the soft, salty balls melted on his tongue.

He was at the movies, eating popcorn, with his friends. What more could he ask?

Cheesy advertisements for the local dentist, a mortgage broker and a delicious if inauthentic looking Mexican restaurant gave way to movie previews. The first was about an alien invasion, massive black ships hovering over cities. He was leaning over, checking to see whether it had coaxed Craig out of his nerves, when he felt a hot breath against his jowl.

"What in Oogla's name are you three playing at?" Drablux hissed.

A second preview played, a comedy this time. Set in an over the top, all male cabaret bar. "We just wanted to go to the movies, for real. That's all."

The lights dimmed once more, fading almost to black, and the screen flashed a message, preparing them for the feature presentation. Drablux scoffed, and Glixor brought forth his inner Bogart.

"And then we saw you here, with Fabian, and I realised we weren't so different. That we both wanted the same thing, to be here, right now. With our friends."

"So, this is my offer."

"Your offer? Glixor, I don't know what kind of leverage you think you have–"

Bogart whispered in his ear: *Keep pushing, Kid. Don't take a backward step!* So he didn't. He spread his mandibles and cut her off.

"I know neither of us are meant to be here right now. So how about we all enjoy the movie, then we let you catch us. Take us back. We'll even keep Fabian a secret. If you promise to put things back to normal." Glixor slurped another mouthful of his drink, and savoured the almost painful sweetness, the delightful bite of the bubbles on the back of his throat. His heart pounded. "Deal?"

The screen went white, and a cheeky desk lamp jumped across the screen. He wasn't quite sure how a desk lamp could be cheeky, but it was. It launched itself onto a letter 'I' and jumped on it, squishing it down flat, before peering out into the audience. He could have sworn that it smiled.

"You come quietly, as soon as the movie's over, and you keep your mandibles clamped about everything you've seen here,"

Drablux paused, as if considering just how far she could go, "I reckon I could make this all blow over in a couple of months. Hell, with Fabian's help, and if you behave yourselves, I reckon I could make an excursion to the cinema a regular thing within four. And get the three of you on set within six."

Glixor glared straight forward, too scared to move, in case he discovered he was dreaming. The lamp faded away, and was replaced by a toy cowboy, arms flopping and flailing as a young human boy laughed and twirled. The movie was animated, unlike any animation Glixor had seen before, but the boy's smile was so wide it was infectious. Over the top of the opening credits, a jaunty little piano played, filling the cinema with a palpable warmth.

You got a friend in me...

"What do you say, Glix? We got a deal?"

You got a friend in me...

"Drablux," Glixor slipped his hands into his pockets as if he was wearing a trenchcoat, late one night on a mist shrouded runway, "I think this is the beginning of a beautiful friendship."

About the author

Thomas is an Australian engineer, writer, and reader with too many books on the shelf waiting to be read and too many ideas scribbled illegibly in notebooks waiting to be written. When he's not staying up too late (sometimes writing, more often procrastinating) he can be found eating vegemite toast, watching old sci-fi shows, or getting far too invested in the footy (that's Australian rules football for the internationals).

Thomas lives in Melbourne with his partner and their dog. He writes (almost) every day flitting between crowd sourced flash fiction experiments, science fiction short stories, strange, unsellable novellas, thriller-leaning novels and the occasional unfinished, untitled fantasy epic. Most of which can be found on his website: thomaskslee.com

Thank you for reading *A Symmetrically Tentacled Friendship*

I hope you enjoyed reading it as much as I loved writing it. If you think others will enjoy *A Symmetrically Tentacled Friendship* too, then please consider leaving a review. Reviews help show readers that picking up a copy of *A Symmetrically Tentacled Friendship* is worth their valuable time. They make a bigger difference than you may realise.

*Review Now at
Goodreads*

Get In Touch

If you have a question, want to suggest a topic or character for my next flash fiction adventure, or just want to say hello, then this is the place to go. You can send me a message direct, or sign-up for my monthly newsletter. I'd love to hear from you!

Get In Touch